THE POETRY BUS

Precious Gems

Edited By Lynsey Evans

First published in Great Britain in 2024 by:

YoungWriters® Est. 1991

Young Writers
Remus House
Coltsfoot Drive
Peterborough
PE2 9BF
Telephone: 01733 890066
Website: www.youngwriters.co.uk

All Rights Reserved
Book Design by Ashley Janson
© Copyright Contributors 2024
Softback ISBN 978-1-83565-563-4
Printed and bound in the UK by BookPrintingUK
Website: www.bookprintinguk.com
YB0596G

FOREWORD

Welcome to a fun-filled book of poems!

Here at Young Writers we are delighted to introduce The Poetry Bus. Pupils could choose to write an acrostic, sense poem or riddle to introduce them to the world of poetry. Giving them this framework allowed the young writers to open their imaginations to a range of topics of their choice, and encouraged them to include other poetic techniques such as similes and descriptive vocabulary.

From family and friends, to animals and places, these pupils have shaped and crafted their ideas brilliantly, showcasing their budding creativity in verse.

We live and breathe creativity here at Young Writers – it gives us life! We want to pass our love of the written word onto the next generation and what better way to do that than to celebrate their writing by publishing it in a book!

Each awesome little poet in this book should be super proud of themselves! We hope you will delight in these poems as much as we have.

CONTENTS

Beaconsfield Primary School, Southall

Muhammad Haris (6)	1
Musa Baksh Chohan (6)	2
Aydan Mohamed (6)	3
Alicia Cardoso (5)	4
Ruginth Jeyaruban (6)	5
Yasmin Hussein (6)	6

Christ Church C of E Primary School, North Shields

Grace Ward-Irving (7)	7
Forest Armstrong Adams (7)	8
Rozalia Kulik (7)	9
Lucas Sloan (6)	10
Edward Hardy (7)	11
Harry Brown (6)	12
Lola Taylor (6)	13
Esmay Cordes (6)	14
Jessica Ohene Odame (6)	15
Lola Jackson (7)	16
Beth Robson (6)	17

Forge Integrated Primary School, Belfast

Oscar D'Arconte (6)	18
Rory Irvine (6)	19
Woody Redden (7)	20
Amaia Ward (7)	21
Frankie Alcorn (7)	22
Rory Browne (6)	23
Jonah Hamilton-Robinson (7)	24
Harrison Campbell (7)	25

Olivia Aston (7)	26
Hugo Curado (7)	27
Luke Steward (7)	28
Lily Benson (7)	29
Alfie Simpson (7)	30
Ellie Thompson (7)	31
Finley Browne (7)	32
Liam Maketo (7)	33
Samuel Jennings (6)	34
Maxwell Downey (6)	35
Leah McDermott (6)	36
Holly Mckinney (7)	37
Luka Byrne (7)	38

Gors Community School, Cockett

Weronika Adach (7)	39
Xueqi (6)	40

Hilltop Primary School, Frindsbury

Maisie Bartholomew (7)	41
Aksara Saththiyaraj (7)	42
Mabel Sterling (6)	43
Avi Chahal (6)	44

Hindley Junior And Infant School, Wigan

Natalia Merkouri (5)	45

Ingfield Manor School, Billingshurst

Lions Class	46

Mount Street Primary School, Greenbank

Wed (6)	47
Sochikaima Ebinaso (5)	48
Emily Ricketts (5)	49

Mundesley Infant School, Mundesley

Artie Perks (5)	50
Arthur Pateman (7)	51
Bella Oakley (7)	52
Reggie Cotter (6)	53

Newbury Park Primary School, Ilford

Rudransh Gangisetty (6)	54
Ajwa Anas (7)	56
Suleiman Joumun (6)	57
Samaira Hayat (7)	58
Lamisah Rahman (7)	59
Karvalli Josiah-Baker (7)	60
Leon Peka (6)	61
Noah Islam (7)	62
Hadi Fawad (7)	63
Jay Valen Rapaka (7)	64
Ruthvik Hemachandran (6)	65
Dharshan Kannathasan (6)	66
Ria Matharu (7)	67
Nyra Jabbal (7)	68
Mannan Khan (6)	69
Myrah Prem Sharai Manda (6)	70
Arohi Bommanaboina (6)	71
Ersilda (7)	72
Eisa Mohamed Imran (7)	73
Jane Bairagee (7)	74
Rhea Bhor (7)	75
Serena Iqbal (5)	76
Rudra Gupta (6)	77
Zuhair Ahmed (8)	78
Agim Mesut (7)	79
Thivyen Yoganathan (6)	80
Alin Patel (7)	81
Haneefah Hussain (6)	82
Amelia Demian (6)	83
Dua Rashid (6)	84
Aisha Nissan (7)	85
Daivick Mahendran (6)	86
Unaisah Butt (7)	87
Sukriti Monoara Bhuiyan (6)	88
Mateo Dalaci (6)	89
Suriya Premkumar (6)	90
Gursirat Kaur (5)	91

Priorsford Primary School, Peebles

Arden Kirk (7)	92
William Bunyan (8)	93
Esther Waddell (7)	94
Sophie Curl (7)	95
May Maruri Exposito (7)	96
Findlay Early (7)	97
Isabelle Payne (8)	98
Ellis Brown (7)	99
Frankie Bon (8)	100
Tessa Ryan (7)	101
Ben Noble (7)	102
Maja McDonald (7)	103
Sofia Gilchrist (7)	104
Ellie Payne (8)	105
Ava Lau-Jones (7)	106
Jackson Hall (7)	107
Hannah Lesilse (8)	108
Olivia Wood (7)	109
Blair Smith (7)	110

Ravensfield Primary School, Dukinfield

Erin Logan (7)	111
Zulaikha Javaid (7)	112
Daisy Winslow Pownall (7)	113
Esme-Grace Bennett	114
Penelope Crosby (7)	115
Heidi Scott	116

Name	Number
Corah Bancroft (7)	117
Ember Phoenix Jeffs (7)	118
Billy Larsen (5)	119
Harper (6)	120
Isabelle Holtby (5)	121
Isabel Dunworth (5)	122
Scarlett Taylor (6)	123
Isla Power (7)	124
Freddie K	125
Ellie Trafford (6)	126
Grace Porritt (5)	127
Eva Thompson (6)	128
Elsie-Mae McDermott (7)	129
Nelly Mlodystach (5)	130
Emelyn Loughman (7)	131
Blake Ashton (7)	132
James Robinson-Higginbotham (5)	133
Darcy Wrigley (5)	134
Rosie Turner (6)	135
Masheea Mahmood (7)	136
Millie Klavon (5)	137
Seren	138
Ivy Egerton (6)	139
Zach Miller (5)	140
Gauta Nthwesane (6)	141
Adanio Vunge	142
Lola Adshead (6)	143
Rose Broomfield Briggs (6)	144
Carla Pereira	145
Jaxon Evans-White (5)	146

THE POEMS

Untitled

I like water,
The shallow, tickly, hot kind,
The transparent, splashy, cold kind,
Surfing on the waves,
Sailing in the sea,
I do like water.

Muhammad Haris (6)
Beaconsfield Primary School, Southall

Untitled

I like water,
The cold, wet, splashy kind,
The bubbly, trickly, hot kind,
Surfing on the waves,
Fishing in the pond,
I do like water.

Musa Baksh Chohan (6)
Beaconsfield Primary School, Southall

Water

I like water,
The white, wet, warm kind,
The blue, bubbly, splashy kind,
Splashing in the bath,
Diving in the pool,
I do like water.

Aydan Mohamed (6)
Beaconsfield Primary School, Southall

Untitled

I like water,
The wet, bubbly, splashy kind,
The deep, tickly, cold kind,
Surfing on the waves,
Diving in the pool,
I do like water.

Alicia Cardoso (5)
Beaconsfield Primary School, Southall

Untitled

I like water,
The warm, wet, white kind,
The bubbly, splashy, deep kind,
Swimming in the sea,
Diving in the pool,
I do like water.

Ruginth Jeyaruban (6)
Beaconsfield Primary School, Southall

Water

I like water
The warm, wet, wavy kind
The bubbly, blue, shallow kind
Swimming in the sea
Diving in the pond
I do like water.

Yasmin Hussein (6)
Beaconsfield Primary School, Southall

My Perfect Pancake

Dripping chocolate sauce,
Juicy sweet strawberries,
Drippy caramel sauce,
Juicy lovely grapes,
Melting multicoloured ice cream,
Toffee sweet sauce, squirty cream,
Drizzling honey, soft bananas.

Grace Ward-Irving (7)
Christ Church C of E Primary School, North Shields

My Perfect Pancake

Crispy sugar on my pancake
And don't forget the custard
Exploding with syrup
Like an erupting volcano
Topped with sweets
Enough sweets to fill an Egyptian tomb
It is nice with vanilla, too.

Forest Armstrong Adams (7)
Christ Church C of E Primary School, North Shields

My Perfect Pancake

Thick and tasty chocolate spread,
Covered all over the top,
A crumbly chocolate flake,
Sprinkled around the edges,
Sticky, sweet caramel,
Drizzled on the bottom layer.

Rozalia Kulik (7)
Christ Church C of E Primary School, North Shields

My Perfect Pancake

Sweet, sweet honey dripping everywhere,
Splashing coconut milk and whipped cream on it,
Chocolate spread,
Does the trick,
My perfect pancake will be as perfect as can be.

Lucas Sloan (6)
Christ Church C of E Primary School, North Shields

My Perfect Pancake

Lovely grapes with dripping chocolate down the pancake
The bacon about to fall off the plate
Drippy butter on the grapes to the bananas
With lovely vanilla ice cream.

Edward Hardy (7)
Christ Church C of E Primary School, North Shields

My Perfect Pancake

Hot and fresh from the pan,
Fresh pancakes,
Sprinkled with sugar,
And sticky toffee sauce,
Sweet strawberries with lemon juice.

Harry Brown (6)
Christ Church C of E Primary School, North Shields

My Perfect Pancake

Dripping honey,
Powdered sugar,
Shiny strawberries,
Juicy blueberries,
Melting butter,
This is a pancake.

Lola Taylor (6)
Christ Church C of E Primary School, North Shields

My Perfect Pancake

Toffee sauce is yummy on pancakes,
Yummy pancakes,
Sprinkles and butter,
Squirty cream, yummy,
Squirty cream.

Esmay Cordes (6)
Christ Church C of E Primary School, North Shields

My Perfect Pancake

Warm and fresh pancakes,
Sprinkle with powdered sugar,
Juicy, round blueberries,
Dressed with sticky honey.

Jessica Ohene Odame (6)
Christ Church C of E Primary School, North Shields

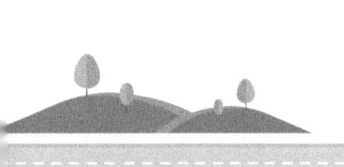

My Perfect Pancake

Dripping strawberries
Beautiful bananas
Falling, drizzling syrup
Warm melted chocolate
Toffee sauce dripping off the top.

Lola Jackson (7)
Christ Church C of E Primary School, North Shields

My Perfect Pancake

Chocolate dripping down the pancake,
Juicy strawberries,
Sprinkled with crunchy sugar.

Beth Robson (6)
Christ Church C of E Primary School, North Shields

Wednesday

W is for Wednesday; that is her name.
E is for eerie because that is what she is.
D is for dangerous games that she likes to play.
N is for night-time; better than day.
E is for electrocuting; Pugsley when she can.
S is for scary things that she likes.
D is for dress; she doesn't do pink.
A is for archery; you will never beat her.
Y is for young because she is only a kid.

Oscar D'Arconte (6)
Forge Integrated Primary School, Belfast

Tommo And Cin

T homas is my big brother
O h what a brilliant boy is he
M aking trades with others
M akes him so kind to me
O h how he misses Cinnamon.

A nd Cinnamon is our cat
N ow that time came to an end
D isappeared from our lives did she.

C innamon was a beautiful cat
I loved her very much
N ow she lives forever in our hearts...

Rory Irvine (6)
Forge Integrated Primary School, Belfast

Super Sonic

S onic is super fast
U niverse far away was his home
P al is called Tails
E ats chilli dogs
R obotnik is his enemy

S onic is a hedgehog
O nly Amy Rose kisses him
N ot Shadow, they are rivals
I think Sonic is super cool because his
C olour is blue!

Woody Redden (7)
Forge Integrated Primary School, Belfast

Unicorns

U nicorns are heaven-sent
N o evil unto them is meant
I t's their love so true and pure
C reating all this love so sure
O f all the creatures big and small
R eaching out to one and all
N ever let them leave your mind
S oon you'll see they're one of a kind.

Amaia Ward (7)
Forge Integrated Primary School, Belfast

Gymnastics

G ymnastics is cool
Y ou would love it too
M y mummy comes to watch
N ew skills every week
A handstand is the best
S ometimes there is a test
T he teacher is fantastic
I love gymnastics
C artwheels are funny
S ometimes you land on your tummy.

Frankie Alcorn (7)
Forge Integrated Primary School, Belfast

Nintendo

N intendo is my favourite game,
I t's really fun to play,
N ow I can beat my dad at it,
T hen he tries again another day.
E nding up in first place,
N ew levels every day,
D riving to collect more coins,
O h, I've won! Hooray!

Rory Browne (6)
Forge Integrated Primary School, Belfast

Fun Ball

F un is being with my friends
O utside in the sun
O pportunities to impress
T ime to get started
B alls begin to bounce
A ll my friends are happy
L et's go have some fun
L aughing all the way home.

Jonah Hamilton-Robinson (7)
Forge Integrated Primary School, Belfast

Football

F un playing football
O utstanding pass
O ffside is a rule
T raining is important
B est team ever is City
A wesome teammates
L ong passes to each other
L ots of fun.

Harrison Campbell (7)
Forge Integrated Primary School, Belfast

Olivia

O h, what a kind girl I am
L oving and happy every day
I ntelligent girl, my teachers say
V ery pretty with long hair
I love my family and my friends
A n acrostic poem all about me!

Olivia Aston (7)
Forge Integrated Primary School, Belfast

Animals

A ardvarks eat ants
N arwhals live under the ice
I guanas are cold-blooded
M oths are nocturnal
A nts are eaten by aardvarks
L lamas can hum
S quid have three hearts.

Hugo Curado (7)
Forge Integrated Primary School, Belfast

Moomie

M y most favourite toy.
O nly Moomie will do.
O vernight, he sleeps with me in bed.
M oomie goes everywhere with me.
I t is the softest toy I have.
E very day, I give him a hug.

Luke Steward (7)
Forge Integrated Primary School, Belfast

Spring Fun

S pring flowers start to bloom,
P laying outside with friends,
R iding bikes and scooters,
I ce cream cones and sprinkles,
N ew lambs are born,
G etting ready for Easter fun!

Lily Benson (7)
Forge Integrated Primary School, Belfast

Healthy

H ealth is important
E at lots of fruit and vegetables
A nd exercise
L ittle sugar
T ake care of yourself
H ave plenty of sleep
Y ou will grow big and strong.

Alfie Simpson (7)
Forge Integrated Primary School, Belfast

Ellie

E very day brings joy so sweet
L aughing with friends, a delightful treat
L ittle moments, big smiles
I magining adventures that go for miles
E very hug feels warm and complete.

Ellie Thompson (7)
Forge Integrated Primary School, Belfast

Yoshi

Y oshi is an adventurous cat,
O ut and about he plays all night,
S leeping in the day, he loves to do,
H e loves treats and strokes under his chin,
I love my cat, Yoshi.

Finley Browne (7)
Forge Integrated Primary School, Belfast

Roblox

R unning through games
O nline fun for me
B uying avatar
L ots of friends to play with
O pen to girls and boys
X box and phone games.

Liam Maketo (7)
Forge Integrated Primary School, Belfast

Mum And Dad

M y friends and I play games
Yo **U** are happy
M um is fun.

D ad is cool
A ria is playing with me
D ad is fun.

Samuel Jennings (6)
Forge Integrated Primary School, Belfast

Guitar

G o to lesson,
U sing strings,
I like to play,
T homas is my teacher,
A n electric guitar,
R ock music.

Maxwell Downey (6)
Forge Integrated Primary School, Belfast

Spot

S pot is very cute.
P laying fetch is his favourite thing.
O ther dogs like to play with him.
T he park is his happy place.

Leah McDermott (6)
Forge Integrated Primary School, Belfast

Cats

C razy when they are playing
A sleep all day long
T hey are furry
S o cuddly like my Murry.

Holly Mckinney (7)
Forge Integrated Primary School, Belfast

Comic

C ooler than
O ther books
M y favourite thing
I s reading
C omics all day long.

Luka Byrne (7)
Forge Integrated Primary School, Belfast

My Smoothies

I can see big, red strawberries,
I can smell the sweet mango and sour strawberries mixing together,
I can feel the soft, slimy bananas as I chop them up,
I can hear the noisy blender mashing the fruit together,
I can taste the sweet, fruity smoothie,
It is yummy in my tummy.

Weronika Adach (7)
Gors Community School, Cockett

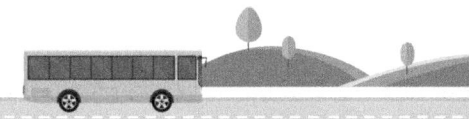

My Smoothie

I can see big strawberries
I can smell the sweet mango
And sour blueberries mixed together
I can feel the soft, slimy banana
As I eat them up
I can taste the sweet fruity smoothie
And it is yummy in my tummy.

Xueqi (6)
Gors Community School, Cockett

Friendship

F riends are kind
R eady to play with me
I love them
E verybody makes new friends
N ever leave someone down, always help them up
D on't make your friends sad or upset them
S chool is more fun with friends
H elp someone when they feel left out
I like having playdates with my friends
P laying sticky toffee is our favourite thing to do.

Maisie Bartholomew (7)
Hilltop Primary School, Frindsbury

The Very Juicy Rainbow Strawberry

My strawberry smells like sweet candy.
My strawberry looks like a rainbow watermelon.
My strawberry tastes like a juicy orange.
My strawberry feels smooth and a little bit bumpy.
My strawberry sounds like summer with a lemonade in my hand.
My strawberry looks like an upside-down watermelon.

Aksara Saththiyaraj (7)
Hilltop Primary School, Frindsbury

I Love Dogs

I love dogs.

L ovely and fluffy
O n the bed, we snuggle
V ery comfy and cosy
E lsie is my dog.

D own the road, we walk
O ver the hills
G etting hot and muddy
S he is my best friend.

Mabel Sterling (6)
Hilltop Primary School, Frindsbury

Shark

S harp teeth open wide
H unt for food sneakily
A nd they are a dangerous creature.
R ough in the deep sea.
K eep yourself safe from the great white
S hark.

Avi Chahal (6)
Hilltop Primary School, Frindsbury

Outside

The sky is bright,
The yellow sun is strong,
And the green grass is lovely.

Natalia Merkouri (5)
Hindley Junior And Infant School, Wigan

The Poetry Bus

We wheeled through the woods on the crunchy path,
We heard these sounds and noises,
The whooshing of the wind,
The chatting of the children,
The vrooming of the aeroplane,
The brumming of the cars,
The sweeping of the leaves,
The banging of the workmen,
The snapping of the twigs,
The rustling of the animals,
We listened to all the sounds and they made us happy.

Lions Class
Ingfield Manor School, Billingshurst

Senses

I smell flowers,
I hear birds singing,
I taste ice cream,
I touch books,
I smell juicy oranges,
I hear children laughing,
I taste yummy cake,
I touch my cat's fur,
I smell green grass,
I hear crickets chirping,
I taste apples,
I touch my hair.

Wed (6)
Mount Street Primary School, Greenbank

The Food Poem

Food is yummy,
Food smells good,
I love food so much,
Food is my favourite,
Food is scrumptious,
But it is very yummy.

Sochikaima Ebinaso (5)
Mount Street Primary School, Greenbank

The Cool Cats

Cool cats will eat a fish,
Next, the cool cats drink milk,
Then they had to work.

Emily Ricketts (5)
Mount Street Primary School, Greenbank

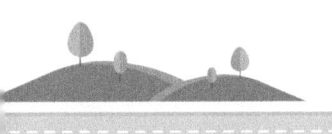

Spitfire And The Bird

Oh look, there's a Spitfire.
It's like a bird.
It's so speedy.
Its wings are like a bird's.
Its nose is like a beak.
The bird is a red kite.
Their wings are so similar.
They both soar through the sky,
It makes me excited!

Artie Perks (5)
Mundesley Infant School, Mundesley

Sea Feelings

I can smell the mammoth sea,
And hear the waves crashing next to me,
I can feel the water,
Splashing my hair,
I can taste the salty air,
I can see a massive wave,
Racing toward me,
Oh, how I love seeing the sea.

Arthur Pateman (7)
Mundesley Infant School, Mundesley

The Dog And The Bog

Once there was a dog, called Fog,
He loved going in the bog!
One day he heard a sound, it was a frog,
Called Sog,
Sog was cold, so Fog
Let him in the house,
Sog said, "You have a lovely home."

Bella Oakley (7)
Mundesley Infant School, Mundesley

My Team

F un and fast
O ur team never last
O n the ball
T ake a shot
B low the whistle
A ll dressed in blue
L et's score
L et's win.

Reggie Cotter (6)
Mundesley Infant School, Mundesley

Splashy Adventures: Dive Into Fun

Splashing in the pool,
I wear my happy grin,
Water hugs me,
Like a friend so kin.
Goggles on my nose,
Like a superhero's gear,
I dive in the pool,
Without a fear.
Rubber duckies cheer me up,
As I float by,
Sunshine paints sparkles,
Up in the sky.
My swimsuit dances,
A watery wave,
In the pool of dreams,
Where laughter never stops.

Each splash a tale that never ends,
In this water world,
I am the pool swirl.
With giggles and splashes,
My day unfolds.
In my pool adventures,
Where joy never holds.
Swimming for kids,
A watery delight.
Nothing beats thrill,
As I swim with pride.

Rudransh Gangisetty (6)
Newbury Park Primary School, Ilford

All About Winter

W inter is cold
I t snows in the cold
N ever gets hot until summer
T he snow is soft
E nds in summer
R iding in summer not winter.

S ummer has finally come
U mbrella we don't need
M um can take me to the park
M um can play with me
E lders can help little ones ride bikes
R emember to have so much fun.

Ajwa Anas (7)
Newbury Park Primary School, Ilford

What Am I?

I fly in the air,
But I have no hair,
I flap my wings,
But I don't sting,
I am beautiful,
But I can't swim in a pool,
I sleep in a cocoon,
But I can't catch a balloon,
I fly and flap my wings,
But a bird goes high over the swings,
I live in leaves,
But the snails chomp on the berries,
I go on trees,
But kids stare at the bees,
While I am a butterfly!

Suleiman Joumun (6)
Newbury Park Primary School, Ilford

A Riddle: Who Am I?

I have a short, fluffy tail,
And large hind legs,
I have two pairs of sharp front teeth,
I have small, furry, long ears,
I can be found in tunnels, burrows and tall grass,
I eat hay and carrots all day,
Through my breakfast, lunch and dinner,
I can be various colours,
Like white, black and brown,
I can run very fast and hop over bushes,
Who am I?

Answer: A bunny.

Samaira Hayat (7)
Newbury Park Primary School, Ilford

Friends

Friends are nice,
Friends are good,
Friends listen to you,
Friends are kind,
Friends have respect,
Friends don't lie,
Friends stay together,
Friends don't run away,
Friends care,
Friends always take care of you,
Friends care for what you say,
Friends don't say bad things,
Friends always play with you,
Friends always hold your hand.

Lamisah Rahman (7)
Newbury Park Primary School, Ilford

The Jumpscare Monster

The monster jelly likes to go into the sewers
To use shortcuts when he commits crimes.
He makes the police go into the sewers
To put him into jail for stealing stuff.
Ruby the monster throws trees with his strength
And throws lampposts at the buildings.
He can jump, high through the sky
So he can make planes explode
So he can burn the city down!

Karvalli Josiah-Baker (7)
Newbury Park Primary School, Ilford

I Show Speed

A donkey is jumping over a bridge
Till he falls in the water
Horse saves the donkey
Till he falls to the ground
"Beep!" says Donkey to the monkey
"To the monkey," says Donkey
"What a good day," says Donkey to Monkey
"Beep," says Horsey to the Lorsy.
"Let's sing," says the monkey to the horsey.

Leon Peka (6)
Newbury Park Primary School, Ilford

Kick Me

"Kick me," said the ball,
"Score, score," said the mall,
"Whoa, whoa," said the bin to the snail,
"Can I talk now?" said the hill,
"What a silly question," said Bill,
"Aren't I in charge?" said the bin,
"Aren't I, aren't I?
Aren't I in charge?" said the bin.

Noah Islam (7)
Newbury Park Primary School, Ilford

A Football Poem

I kick the ball on the pitch
With the sun feeling bright on my face
When I score, I love hearing
Everyone screaming my name and cheering.
Football brings everyone together
Like teamwork.
I see with my eyes
The ball rolling fast in the grass
To be caught and scored by everyone passionately
Football will always be my passion.

Hadi Fawad (7)
Newbury Park Primary School, Ilford

What Am I?

I go very fast.
I have a powerful engine.
I'm faster than regular cars.
I have two doors.
I have two headlights and a rear light.
I have four tyres.
I have one spoiler.
Some of us are electric or petrol.
I have mirrors.
I have an aerodynamic shape.
What am I?

Answer: A supercar.

Jay Valen Rapaka (7)
Newbury Park Primary School, Ilford

Friends

F unny moments we always find.
R unning races, we all won.
I n games, we play and share.
E very day with you, my best friend.
N oisy giggles when you tickle.
D ancing until the day is done.
S illy jokes and secrets we share.

Together forever, a perfect pair!

Ruthvik Hemachandran (6)
Newbury Park Primary School, Ilford

Harvest

H elping others who are hungry
A pples and carrots are healthy treats
R emember to bring a donation to school!
V ery important not to waste food
E veryone can bring one packet of fruits
S ave money by growing your own
T ime to thank the hero farmers.

Dharshan Kannathasan (6)
Newbury Park Primary School, Ilford

Spring

S unshine through my window bright,
P laying in the garden with delight,
R aindrops on the roof go tap, tap, tap,
I n the garden, bugs take a nap,
N ose tickles when I smell flowers,
G iggles and laughter with my little sister for hours.

Ria Matharu (7)
Newbury Park Primary School, Ilford

What Am I?

I fly in the air by fluttering my wings.
I am smaller than your hand.
If you look carefully, you will see that I am many different colours.
For my food, I drink delicious nectar from flowers.
I have six legs and two antennae.
At first, I come out of a cocoon.

Nyra Jabbal (7)
Newbury Park Primary School, Ilford

What Am I?

I have ears
I have fur
I can be black and white
I have cute eyes
Who am I?

Answer: A cat.

I have a tail
I wag my tail
I bark
I play great with the bone
Who am I?

Answer: A dog.

Mannan Khan (6)
Newbury Park Primary School, Ilford

Winter Poem

The sky is dark and the ground is white,
The world is peaceful on this wintry night.
No one around, not a sound to be heard,
Not a laugh, not a car, not even a bird.
For a moment it's just the snow and me,
I smile inside, I feel so free.

Myrah Prem Sharai Manda (6)
Newbury Park Primary School, Ilford

What Am I?

I come in different colours.
But I'm mostly the colour red.
I am the favourite of many kids, and I'm used to prepare dessert.
I wear green caps.
My body is full of eyes.
Tell me, what am I?

Answer: A strawberry.

Arohi Bommanaboina (6)
Newbury Park Primary School, Ilford

Wrong

We went on holiday with Mr Wrong,
Everything we said, he said was wrong.
He asked us if night came before day,
Or day before night?
We said day came before night,
He said, wrong.
So we said night came before day,
He said, wrong.

Ersilda (7)
Newbury Park Primary School, Ilford

Waiting For Snow

W here, where is the snow?
I 'm waiting for the twinkling flakes
N othing comes yet
T ime is running out soon, it is spring
E agerly, I am waiting for you
R eally! There is no snow in 2024.

Eisa Mohamed Imran (7)
Newbury Park Primary School, Ilford

The Sun

T he sun is bright,
H its your eyes because of the light,
E stimate the temperature of the sun.

S ay! How golden the sun is,
U nknown the temperature of the sun,
N ever not bright sun.

Jane Bairagee (7)
Newbury Park Primary School, Ilford

Riddle Poems

I hate dogs
I drink milk
I chase mice
What am I?

Answer: A cat.

I eat leaves
I live in the zoo
I have a very long neck
What am I?

Answer: A giraffe.

Rhea Bhor (7)
Newbury Park Primary School, Ilford

Playground

P laying
L ittle people
A pple
Y oung people
G reen grass
R ound balls
O ranges
U nder the tree
N ature
D ancing.

Serena Iqbal (5)
Newbury Park Primary School, Ilford

Snowman

S unshine is blessings
N ever give up
O ld is gold
W ork hard always
M um is my best friend
A lways trust yourself
N othing is impossible.

Rudra Gupta (6)
Newbury Park Primary School, Ilford

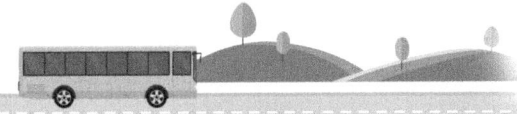

Riddle Poem

I cannot run very fast.
I am the tallest mammal in the world.
I am a herbivorous animal.
I have brown spots on my body.
I eat leaves.
What am I?

Answer: A giraffe.

Zuhair Ahmed (8)
Newbury Park Primary School, Ilford

The Best Snowday Ever

Winter, fluffy snow all around,
Ice skating is fun to do in the snow,
Snowflakes, snowflakes dance all around,
Snowflakes, snowflakes in the air,
Snowflakes, snowflakes everywhere!

Agim Mesut (7)
Newbury Park Primary School, Ilford

The Star

The star looks sparkly,
I took the star,
I spat the star into my jar,
It glows bright,
Never stop the glittering light,
The star will beam,
Only if it's dark.

Thivyen Yoganathan (6)
Newbury Park Primary School, Ilford

Mole And Bear

Mole and Bear were staying over there,
They both didn't care,
Bear and Snake were eating a cake,
Eating a cake,
Eating a cake,
Bear and Snake were eating a cake.

Alin Patel (7)
Newbury Park Primary School, Ilford

Don't Sit On Your Melon Helen!

I love melons,
And my name is Helen,
I eat lots of melons,
So they say,
"Don't sit on your melon, Helen!"
But it was too late,
I sat on my melon!

Haneefah Hussain (6)
Newbury Park Primary School, Ilford

My Cat

I have a pet
She is a cat
Her name is Kitty
She is so pretty
My cat likes milk
It's her favourite drink
She likes dry food
Which is very good.

Amelia Demian (6)
Newbury Park Primary School, Ilford

Beach

S and bucket
A round
N ext
D ig.

B all
E agle
A ir
C rab
H ats.

Dua Rashid (6)
Newbury Park Primary School, Ilford

All About Me

A lways smiles
I s a bit shy
S inging is her thing
H er favourite colour is pink
A ll she does is play around.

Aisha Nissan (7)
Newbury Park Primary School, Ilford

At School

A corn
T ree

S wimming
C ool
H at
O utside
O utside play
L olly.

Daivick Mahendran (6)
Newbury Park Primary School, Ilford

The Red Bus

What's red?
What's bright?
What has two yellow lights?
What's going round and round
Taking us all through the town?

Unaisah Butt (7)
Newbury Park Primary School, Ilford

School

S uper
C ool
H appy
O utdoor play
O n time
L istening.

Sukriti Monoara Bhuiyan (6)
Newbury Park Primary School, Ilford

Untitled

I live in the sea and I am a big mammal.
I am deep blue.
I splash water and splash around.
Who am I?

Mateo Dalaci (6)
Newbury Park Primary School, Ilford

Sunny

S unshine
U p
N ice heat
N ever dark
Y ellow.

Suriya Premkumar (6)
Newbury Park Primary School, Ilford

Sun

S ky
U p
N ice.

Gursirat Kaur (5)
Newbury Park Primary School, Ilford

A Robin In Winter

I hear the crunchy leaves underneath my feet,
I hear the chirping song of a robin,
I see a little brown bird with an orange breast,
I see a beady eye looking at me,
I wish I could feel the silky brown feathers, but I feel cold frosty winter snow,
I smell pine needles,
I smell cold frosty air,
I taste some hot chocolate that's the same shade as the robin,
I taste the cold frosty snow on my tongue.
Winter and the robin are here.

Arden Kirk (7)
Priorsford Primary School, Peebles

Winter And Robins

When I hear the fire crackling
It's the colour of the robin's breast.
When I taste my hot chocolate
It is the same shade as the robin's wings.
I go for a walk and I see my black gloves
They remind me of the robin's eyes.
I touch the smooth snow and
Imagine it, just like a robin, soft and silky.
I smell the pine trees and
Remember where the robins live.

William Bunyan (8)
Priorsford Primary School, Peebles

Winter And Robins

When I
Wake up
In the morning
I hear the robin
Singing in my garden
When I leave my house
I can smell the fire burning
I taste the cold ice as I look
For the robin, when I see the
Robin with its beautiful wings
Out, it makes me feel happy in
And out, when I go to sleep
At night, I imagine touching
Its soft little feathers.

Esther Waddell (7)
Priorsford Primary School, Peebles

The Robin Visits In Winter

I hear
A robin's
Song in the
Frosty garden. I taste
The snow on my tongue
And, when I look up I
See a robin. I see the robin's
Orangey red breast. I wish
I was a robin. I smell pine
Needles in the air. I
Touch the frosty
Leaves and wish
I could touch
The robin's soft
Feathers.

Sophie Curl (7)
Priorsford Primary School, Peebles

The Robin Visits In Winter

I can smell smoke from my home as I walk in my garden looking for the robin.
I hear pine needles crunching under my feet.
I stick my tongue out to taste the snowflakes.
I see a small bird with an orangey tummy.
It is the robin.
When I see a robin, I want to touch its fluffy feathers.
I feel Christmassy.

May Maruri Exposito (7)
Priorsford Primary School, Peebles

The Robins Are Back

I taste the cold watery taste of winter.
I smell all the Christmas smells.
I think of the robins.
If I touched you, you would feel cuddly.
If I touched you, I would feel how soft you were.
If I heard you, it would be a sweet song.
If I saw you, I'd see a red breast with little black eyes.

Findlay Early (7)
Priorsford Primary School, Peebles

A Robin In Winter

Cold frost
Tingling on
My face. I hear
Your chirping song
Dancing towards me. I
See you fluttering away
From me. I can taste the
Frost in the air. I smell
Smoke from the
Chimney and then
I see your red
Breast again.
I am happy
To see the
Robin.

Isabelle Payne (8)
Priorsford Primary School, Peebles

Winter's Robin!

I can touch the smooth, silky feather of a robin.
I can see a tiny brown bird with an orangey-red breast in the garden.
I can taste the sharp crystal ice on my tongue.
I can smell the fire crackling in the wood.
I can hear a robin chirping away.
I feel happy when I see a robin.

Ellis Brown (7)
Priorsford Primary School, Peebles

The Robins Are Back

I smell the frost in the air whilst I look for the robin.
I can taste the crunchy ice in the air.
I see the robin's brown feathers and its orangy red chest.
I hear the robin's song, and I feel happy and Christmassy.
I wish I could feel the robin's fluffy feathers.

Frankie Bon (8)
Priorsford Primary School, Peebles

A Robin In Winter

If I
Could touch you
You would
Be soft and silky.
The smell of warm food
And hot chocolate reminds
Me of you, they taste of winter
I hear pine needles crunching and
The robin's song
I see brown feathers and
A red breast in
The cold.

Tessa Ryan (7)
Priorsford Primary School, Peebles

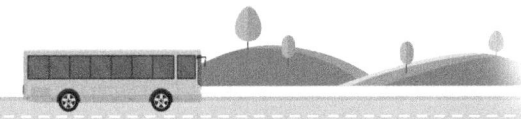

The Robins Are Back!

I see
You fly
In the sky
With your red
Tummy. When I stand
I hear your beautiful
Song. If I could touch
You, you would feel so
Soft to the touch.
If I could smell you,
You would smell so good.
I taste hot chocolate
To warm me up.

Ben Noble (7)
Priorsford Primary School, Peebles

A Robin In Winter

I wish
I could
Touch the
Silky soft feathers
Of a robin.
I smell pine needles and
Think of a robin.
I taste gooey marshmallows
In my hot chocolate.
I hear a robin cheeping and singing.
Finally, I
See a robin on
A branch.

Maja McDonald (7)
Priorsford Primary School, Peebles

Winterland Robins

As I leave my house, I can smell the fire burning.
I hear snow cracking under my feet and the robin's happy song.
I see the orangey-red tummy on the robin.
I taste the cold ice as I look for the robin.
I wish I could touch the robin's fluffy feathers.

Sofia Gilchrist (7)
Priorsford Primary School, Peebles

Winter's Robin

I see a small bird with its feathers puffed up
against the cold air.
I hear your beautiful song cheeping past
me.
I taste the frosty night air
And I smell a warming hot chocolate.
I dream of touching your feathers,
They are silky smooth.

Ellie Payne (8)
Priorsford Primary School, Peebles

Winter Robin

I can see a small brown bird with an orangey-red breast
I can hear a robin chirping loudly
I can taste snow in my mouth, watery and icy
I can smell the winter air
I wish I could touch a delicate, soft and fluffy robin.

Ava Lau-Jones (7)
Priorsford Primary School, Peebles

The Robins Are Back

I see the beady eyes looking at me,
I hear the tweeting in the cold air,
I taste the coldness of the night,
I want to touch the robin's red breast,
It would feel smooth,
I smell smoke coming out of a chimney.

Jackson Hall (7)
Priorsford Primary School, Peebles

Robins

I can
Smell the
Fire burning
Taste the snow
On my tongue. I can
Hear the robin singing
A song. I can see the
Robin staring at me
With its beady eye
I wish I could touch
Their feathers.

Hannah Lesilse (8)
Priorsford Primary School, Peebles

Winter's Robin

I can smell the fire burning,
I can taste the snow on my tongue,
I can hear the robin singing a song,
I can see the robin staring at me,
I wish I could touch its soft fluffy feathers.

Olivia Wood (7)
Priorsford Primary School, Peebles

A Robin In Winter

I see a robin on a tree branch
I hear the robin singing songs
I smell winter coming soon
I taste the snowflakes on my tongue
I feel happy to see a robin.

Blair Smith (7)//
Priorsford Primary School, Peebles

My Favourite Person

B londe, silky hair all day,
R eading two times faster than me,
I love her and she loves me, because we're besties,
E asy writing, she is great,
A playdate is okay anytime,
N ice words, she loves every say,
N ice friend all day,
A black coat is fine, she wears black.

Erin Logan (7)
Ravensfield Primary School, Dukinfield

Zulaikha Javaid

Z ulaikha is super
U nique and not rude
L ikeable
A lways pretty
I ncredible
K ind
H appy always
A mazing.

J azzy
A wesome
V icious
A lways playing
I nexplainable
D ifferent.

Zulaikha Javaid (7)
Ravensfield Primary School, Dukinfield

Daisy Winslow

D elightful
A mazing
I ntelligent
S uper
Y ou are incredible.

W onderful
I n Class 4
N ice
S mart
L ovely
O nly Daisy in C4
W izard lover.

Daisy Winslow Pownall (7)
Ravensfield Primary School, Dukinfield

My Favourite Person

She is a kind friend and is always playing with me
And she is always talking to me
And has sparkly, pretty, beautiful green eyes
And she has beautiful, pink, rosy cheeks
And she always has a plait and pink lips
And she always smiles.

Esme-Grace Bennett
Ravensfield Primary School, Dukinfield

My Favourite Person

I mogen is an amazing person and super loving
M y best friend
O n top of the world
G reat dancer and singer
E yes that are amazing, blue and sparkle like the sun
N ever late for anything.

Penelope Crosby (7)
Ravensfield Primary School, Dukinfield

My Favourite Person

C aring and beautiful as can be.
O kay, my friend and beautiful, rosy cheeks.
R ed cardigan and River Island boots.
A lways being good and listening to Miss Brooks.
H eidi's very good friend.

Heidi Scott
Ravensfield Primary School, Dukinfield

My Favourite Person

I mogen is the best
M y favourite is absolutely her!
O h my gosh, she is the prettiest girl
G lowing, nice girl!
E yes... her eyes are freedom!
N o way you're taking her.

Corah Bancroft (7)
Ravensfield Primary School, Dukinfield

Ember Jeffs

E xcellent
M ind reader
B eautiful
E mber's very kind
R eally kind.

J oyful
E xcellent at reading
F unny
F un
S miley.

Ember Phoenix Jeffs (7)
Ravensfield Primary School, Dukinfield

Harper

H arper is beautiful
A nd her eyes are blue
R eptiles are Harper's favourite
P ets are Harper's favourite
E very day, she makes me smile
R eally good friend.

Billy Larsen (5)
Ravensfield Primary School, Dukinfield

Billy

B illy has brown hair
I always see Billy working hard
L ike him lots, he's funny!
L ikes to make everyone happy
Y es, Billy! I want you to play with me.

Harper (6)
Ravensfield Primary School, Dukinfield

Helena

H elena's favourite animal is an
E lephant - they're her favourite
L ovely Helena is kind and
E nergetic
N ice and caring
A lways polite.

Isabelle Holtby (5)
Ravensfield Primary School, Dukinfield

Isabella

I think she is kind
S miley
A lways smiling
B londe hair
E nergetic
L ovely
L ots of laughing
A pink bobble in her hair.

Isabel Dunworth (5)
Ravensfield Primary School, Dukinfield

Phoebe

P owerful Phoebe
H elpful Phoebe
O n the coach, she sits with me
E very day, she plays.
B est friend Phoebe.
E very day, she's smiling.

Scarlett Taylor (6)
Ravensfield Primary School, Dukinfield

Isla Power

I ntelligent
S mart
L oved
A rt lover.

P roud
O nly kind
W onderful
E xcellent
R eally helpful.

Isla Power (7)
Ravensfield Primary School, Dukinfield

Aaliah

A t school, she plays with me
A nd she shares with me
L ovely and kind
I think she is funny
A nd she's excellent
H as brown hair.

Freddie K
Ravensfield Primary School, Dukinfield

My Favourite Person

X ander is so, so, so cute
A wesome baby
N ice eyes
D efinitely cheeky
E llie is his sister
R eally wrecks the bed.

Ellie Trafford (6)
Ravensfield Primary School, Dukinfield

Darcey

D arcey is kind and happy
A round the playground
R osy cheeks
C alm and happy
E very day, she is kind
Y outhful.

Grace Porritt (5)
Ravensfield Primary School, Dukinfield

My Friend

R osie is very kind
O nly always going to be my best friend forever
S he is happy
I like her eyes
E veryone likes her.

Eva Thompson (6)
Ravensfield Primary School, Dukinfield

Elsie-Mae

E legant
L ovely
S weet
I ntelligent
E xcellent.

M agical
A mazing
E nergetic.

Elsie-Mae McDermott (7)
Ravensfield Primary School, Dukinfield

My Friend

L ayla plays with people
A nd she is very kind
Y ou like to chat to people
L ayla, we love you so much
A bit cheeky.

Nelly Mlodystach (5)
Ravensfield Primary School, Dukinfield

My Favourite Person Is...

A mazing hair.
M arvellous shoes.
I ncredible tights.
L ong hair.
I ncredible spirit.
A mazing writing.

Emelyn Loughman (7)
Ravensfield Primary School, Dukinfield

Duchess

D og
U sually cute
C ute dog
H uggy dog
E yes like two diamonds
S neaky dog
S o cute.

Blake Ashton (7)
Ravensfield Primary School, Dukinfield

Amine

A mine is so kind
M y oldest friend
I s Amine, I think she is
N ice, never sad
E very day, she smiles.

James Robinson-Higginbotham (5)
Ravensfield Primary School, Dukinfield

Fred

He always helps us with phonics.
He always tells us words.
Oats all over his tum.
He is green and black.
Every day, he helps us.

Darcy Wrigley (5)
Ravensfield Primary School, Dukinfield

My Friend

C arla is funny.
A very kind friend.
R osy cheeks.
L ikes to play basketball.
A best friend.

Rosie Turner (6)
Ravensfield Primary School, Dukinfield

Masheea Mahmood

M asheea
A mazing
S uperstar
H elpful to
E veryone
E very day
A lways.

Masheea Mahmood (7)
Ravensfield Primary School, Dukinfield

Charlie

Charlie is kind
When someone's upset, he smiles.
He has got brown eyes.
He has got light skin.
He has pink cheeks.

Millie Klavon (5)
Ravensfield Primary School, Dukinfield

Seren

S uper helper
E at quick
R eally good writer
E ating champion
N ever give up.

Seren
Ravensfield Primary School, Dukinfield

Rose

R ose's skin is peach
O nly is kind
S he spies on everybody
E yes are blue.

Ivy Egerton (6)
Ravensfield Primary School, Dukinfield

Laken

L aken is fast
A lways
K ind
E very day, he makes me laugh
N ice.

Zach Miller (5)
Ravensfield Primary School, Dukinfield

Gauta

G rateful
A wesome
U nderstanding
T alented
A mazing.

Gauta Nthwesane (6)
Ravensfield Primary School, Dukinfield

Sara

S ara is kind
A nna is Sara's sister
R eally kind
A ce.

Adanio Vunge
Ravensfield Primary School, Dukinfield

Lola

L oving
O nly Lola in Class 4
L oves to help
A mazing.

Lola Adshead (6)
Ravensfield Primary School, Dukinfield

Ivy

I vy is good at singing and
V ery helpful
Y ou smell good.

Rose Broomfield Briggs (6)
Ravensfield Primary School, Dukinfield

My Friend

E va is good
V ery friendly
A lways good at phonics.

Carla Pereira
Ravensfield Primary School, Dukinfield

My Friend

D estiny is joking
E xpert at PE
S he is helpful.

Jaxon Evans-White (5)
Ravensfield Primary School, Dukinfield

YOUNG WRITERS INFORMATION

We hope you have enjoyed reading this book – and that you will continue to in the coming years.

If you're the parent or family member of an enthusiastic poet or story writer, do visit our website **www.youngwriters.co.uk/subscribe** and sign up to receive news, competitions, writing challenges and tips, activities and much, much more! There's lots to keep budding writers motivated!

If you would like to order further copies of this book, or any of our other titles, then please give us a call or order via your online account.

Young Writers
Remus House
Coltsfoot Drive
Peterborough
PE2 9BF
(01733) 890066
info@youngwriters.co.uk

Join in the conversation!
Tips, news, giveaways and much more!

- YoungWritersUK
- YoungWritersCW
- youngwriterscw
- youngwriterscw